ENCHANTED NIGHT

Other Books by
STEVEN MILLHAUSER

STEVEN MILLHAUSER

A NOVELLA

ENCHANTED NIGHT

 CROWN PUBLISHERS NEW YORK

Published by Crown Publishers, 201 East 50th Street, New York, New York 10022. Member of the Crown Publishing Group.

Random House, Inc. New York, Toronto, Sydney, Auckland
www.randomhouse.com

CROWN is a trademark and the Crown colophon is a registered trademark of Random House, Inc.

Design by K. Minster

Printed in the United States of America

Library of Congress Cataloging-in-Publication Data
Millhauser, Steven.
      Enchanted night / by Steven Millhauser.—1st ed.
      I. Title.
   PS3563.I422E53   1999
   813'.54—dc21   99-25517
                                                 CIP

ISBN 0-609-60516-X

10 9 8 7 6 5 4 3 2 1

First Edition

Thou that mak'st a day of night,
Goddesse, excellently bright.

ENCHANTED NIGHT

RESTLESS

A hot summer night in southern Connecticut, tide going out and the moon still rising. Laura Engstrom, fourteen years old, sits up in bed and throws the covers off. Her forehead is damp, her hair feels wet. Through the screens of the two half-open windows she can hear a rasp of crickets and a dim rush of traffic on the distant thruway. Five past twelve. Do you know where your children are? The room is so hot that the heat is a hand gripping her throat. Got to move, got to do something. Moonlight is streaming in past the edges of the closed and slightly raised venetian blinds. She can't breathe in this room, in this house. Oh man, do something. Do it. The crickets are growing louder. A smell of cut grass mixes with a salt tang of low tide from the beach four blocks away. She imagines herself out there, on the night beach, low waves breaking, crunch of sand, the lifeguard chairs tall and white and clean under the moon, but the thought disturbs her—she feels exposed, a girl in moonlight, out in the open, spied on. She doesn't want anyone to look at her. No one is allowed to think about her body. But she can't stay in her room, oh no. If she doesn't do something right away, this second, she'll scream. The inside of her skin itches. Her bones itch. So how do you scratch your bones? Laura steps onto the braided throw rug beside her bed and pulls on her jeans. They are so tight that she has to suck in her flat stomach to get the hole over the copper button. She pulls off her nightgown and puts on a white T-shirt—no bra—and a denim jacket with a lump in one pocket: half a roll of Life Savers. She has to get out of there, she has to breathe. If you don't breathe, you're dead. The room is killing her. She won't go far.

CHORUS OF NIGHT VOICES

This is the night of revelation. This is the night the dolls wake. This is the night of the dreamer in the attic. This is the night of the piper in the woods.

THE MAN IN THE ATTIC

At exactly midnight by his strapless watch, Haverstraw puts down his No. 2 hexagonal yellow pencil beside his spiral-bound notebook, which he leaves open on the desk, and leans back in his chair. For a moment he feels dizzy, and grips the edge of the desk; it is hot in the attic room, and the air feels stale and close, despite the twenty-year-old rattling window fan that is supposed to draw the hot air out and somehow leave coolness in its wake. The attic room, lined with bookshelves, is above the second floor of the house, where his mother has her bedroom. Haverstraw's bedroom is also on the second floor, but he prefers to sleep in the old guest-bed in the attic study. The mattress sags, his feet stick over the end, and the room is poorly heated in winter, but Haverstraw does not seek comfort. Haverstraw is thirty-nine years old and lives with his sixty-six-year-old mother. For the last nine years he has been at work on an immense project, an experiment in memory, which will justify him. Tonight the writing has gone well, or at least not badly, though perhaps his ideas have carried him a little astray; he has the sudden sense that the whole project is astray, his whole life astray, but the thought is so terrifying that he quickly suppresses it. He must get out and walk in the night. His waking hours are divided into three segments: from one in the afternoon to six at night he gets through the day, from seven to midnight he writes, and from midnight to five in the morning he gets through the night. He sleeps from five in the morning to one in the afternoon. Dinner with his mother is from six to seven—always. His work will justify him. People will understand. He will be redeemed. Remember old Haverstraw? Guy who lived in the attic? Well! Seems that he. Turns out he. Haverstraw needs to get outside and walk. He turns off the bent-neck standing lamp, pushes back his chair—an old kitchen chair with a pillow on the seat—and stands up, wondering whether his little attacks of dizziness are something he ought to worry about. After all, he's a man almost forty, a man stuck in a bog. His back hurts. His eyes burn. His life hurts. He will be justified. He picks up his watch without a strap and thrusts it into his pocket. Haverstraw crosses the room, switches off the overhead light, and makes his way through the unfinished part of the attic, filled with the abandoned games of his adolescence, the stuffed animals of his childhood. He never throws anything out. Somewhere in a shoebox are all the little prizes from the cereal boxes of thirty years ago, still in their transparent crinkly plastic wrappers. In a drawer of the old dresser sit piles of old bubblegum cards no one has ever heard of: science-fiction cards, movie-star cards, fire-engine cards. He still has his old patrol-boy badge on its white strap, his old paper targets full of BB holes. He ought to clear out all this junk, but it would be like throwing away his childhood. Haverstraw tiptoes down the wooden steps of the attic and makes his way in the dark along the second-floor hall, past his sleeping mother—he can hear her breathing—and down the carpeted stairs. On the dark landing he passes a black, invisible picture: Hokusai's *Great Wave*. In his mind he sees vividly the little yellow boats, the little white heads, the towering waves that frightened him as a child, and far away the wave-like top of Mount Fuji. He continues down the carpeted stairs to the front hall. From a hook on the wobbly clothestree he removes his blue nylon windbreaker. He opens the front door quietly, for his mother is a light sleeper. When he steps outside he sees, high up in the dark blue sky, the big white summer moon. His heart lifts. The night will forgive him.

THE DREAM
OF THE MANNEQUIN

In the department-store window on Main Street, the mannequin stands in her night beauty. Her dark green sunglasses, black in the red-lit window, reveal their secret: they are a form of jewelry, which she wears solely to heighten the elegance of her small, delicate nose and well-cut lips, to give her an air of alluring mystery. Her pale summer dress, soft as rose petals, clings to her slender hips and her long, long legs, one of which stands a little in front of the other. She is wearing a white straw hat, broad-brimmed and tilted at an angle, and white leather sandals. As the stoplight changes from red to green, her hard, satiny skin gives off a glow now red, now green. One bare arm is raised before her, the fingers gracefully extended, in a gesture that in an ordinary person might be a sign of greeting, but that, in her, closes the perfect circle of her self-absorption. The rigor of her pose stimulates in the mannequin a secret desire: she dreams of release, of the dropping of her guard, of the voluptuous fall into motion. Sometimes it seems to her that she is simply waiting—waiting for the moment when she will be able to relax her will a little. Then the beautiful arm will begin to fall, her grave immobility will melt into motion. In the instant of that unthinkable swoon, all will change: she will leave herself behind forever. And at this thought, which makes her legs tingle, a new rigor of wariness comes over her, for the one thing she must never do is give herself away.

OUTLAWS

As Haverstraw steps out from under the thruway overpass, on his way to Mrs. Kasco's, he sees something moving in the black trees beside the low white-brick building set back discreetly from the road. Haverstraw thinks of it as the Whatchamacallit Building, though he knows it is the corporate headquarters of a manufacturer of ball bearings. He remembers when the land was a wooded lot between the thruway embankment and a back yard with a picnic table. Light from lampposts in the parking lot falls dimly on the trees, leaving black, inviting clumps of shadow, and Haverstraw wonders whether he sees the figure of a girl disappearing into the dark. He thinks of the outlaw band that has been preying on the town: a gang of high school girls, five or six of them, who break into houses at night, take food from kitchens, and steal small, unimportant objects like refrigerator magnets, toothbrushes, and eyeglass cases. They always leave a note penciled in neat capital letters: WE ARE YOUR DAUGHTERS The girls are sly and very well prepared: they enter through unlocked back doors or cellar windows, make their way noiselessly into the house, and always sit in the living room before slipping away. Once three of them were seen gliding through a dark kitchen, but when the woman who was sitting in her kitchen at one o'clock in the morning with a glass of Johnnie Walker Red rose screaming and turned on the light, the girls had vanished. The mothers of the town are anxious, and call the police frequently, but Haverstraw is interested: he envies the girls their freedom, their boldness, their pleasure in violation, their habit of irony. He hopes they will invade his house and steal things.

THE WINDOW

Half-past twelve on the digital clock, which casts a blue tint on her hair on the pillow. Janet Manning, twenty years old, wakes up suddenly in her big bedroom on the second floor. A pebble has struck the window. Has a pebble struck her window? She hurries over to the window beside her dark desk with its sagging beachbag, raises the shade, and looks down into the moonlit back yard. The rope swing hangs from the silver maple. In the yard, moon-bright and empty, there's only the shadow of the garage and the brilliant bluish green of the moonlit grass. So green, the grass, so strangely moonly green, that it looks greener than green: silk-blouse green, eyelid green, the green of transparent childhood marbles rolling in sun and shade. There was no plan, no agreement, and yet standing on the beach with a white towel around his neck he had looked at her a certain way and said: I can't wait till tomorrow. And she had said: Then don't!—and laughed. Stupid laugh! The laugh of a complete idiot! He is so beautiful to her that the thought of his cheekbone shining with water in sunlight makes her want to cry out. Nervously she runs a hand through her hair, jerks it away. Her hair is a disaster. Better go back to bed, pull the sheet over your head, live alone, die alone, but she stays kneeling at the window, drowsy-awake, wistful. The night reminds her of a painting, the one that's all blue night sky with a big white moon at the top, and near the bottom a clown in a white costume. Snow-cool light, the air clear blue and still—and as she looks down into the hush of the yard, suddenly she is six years old, looking down into the same yard, glittering with new snow under the brilliant winter moon.

THE PIPER IN THE WOODS

From the woods in the north part of town there rises a sound of flute music, dark and sweet. It rises in slow ripples, falls, in slow ripples it rises, again falls, a tireless slow rising and falling, insistent, a dark call, a languorous fall. Perhaps it is only birdsong, there in the dark trees.

ON THE HILL

On the wooded slope behind the white brick building, the leader of the gang stops for a moment, her head cocked to one side, her left hand raised. She is a tall girl, long-boned, lean-muscled, narrow-hipped, dressed in tight jeans and a hooded black sweatshirt, her blond hair short and thick and combed back on both sides behind her ears. From an elastic string around her neck hangs a black eye-mask, which she will slip on when she enters a yard. In her pocket she carries a pen knife, which she is prepared to use against any attacker. She will never allow herself to be unmasked. Her name is Linda Harris, but she calls herself Summer Storm. The other girls, all in jeans and hooded black sweatshirts, stop below her, alert, their arms tense, their heads raised. Summer Storm hears something far away, a dim music, rising and falling. It is like something she remembers or is on the verge of remembering. Closer by she hears the sound of footsteps in the gravel of the roadside below. She steps back. Through the leaves she sees the bright white moon in the dark blue sky. Against the moon, close and black and very sharp, stands the single leaf of a sugar maple. They will have to be careful, on this bright night. Summer Storm beckons with her hand, and the band of girls moves on.

LAURA IN MOONLIGHT

In the warm night air, under the dark blue sky, Laura feels soothed: she can breathe now, out in the open, as if the suburban night under the wide sky is a western prairie. She thinks of cowboys in old movies, saddlebags, snorting horses, blankets under the stars. Yep. Ah reckon. No sidewalks here—she walks along the edge of the road, under streetlights arching out from telephone poles. In the tangerine-colored light she watches her shadow stretching out longer and longer, a taffy girl, a telescope girl. Where to go? Under branches of sugar maples and lindens, heavy with leaf-smell, shot through with moonlight and streetlight, she sees a few leaves that are a glowing and translucent green. Through the glowing leaves she can see shadows of other leaves. Then the sudden stretching-away night sky of the western prairie. Oh bury me not. On the lone pray-reee. Past the ranch houses of her neighborhood, past the lawn sprinklers glimmering in moonlight, past the NO PARKING signs on top of their green metal posts with vertical rows of screw-holes. Oh where? She feels restless and exposed. She needs a place to go to, a place where she can be alone, away from the basketball nets and the little black garage windows, the oil fill-pipes poking up out of front yards and the whitewashed rocks at the lawn's edge—a private place, outside but secret as an attic, where no one can find her. She looks at the moon, up there in the sky. It's almost perfectly round except for one side that looks a little flat and smudged, as if someone has rubbed it with a thumb, and she has a sudden desire to be there, in that blaze of whiteness, looking down unseen at the little town below, the toy houses with their removable chimneys, the little maples and streetlights, the tiny people with their tiny sorrows.

A WOMAN WAITING

Mrs. Kasco, in her gold kimono decorated with red and green dragons, which she picked up on sale in Japantown ten years ago on a visit to her sister in San Francisco, sits in the old armchair smoking a cigarette, drinking a glass of red wine, and reading *Jennie Gerhardt* as she waits for Haverstraw. It's nearly one in the morning and he always visits her on Fridays and Saturdays at one in the morning. She has known Haverstraw since high school, a polite boy with restless eyes who played chess with her son, and she still thinks of him as a kid of seventeen, even though he's thirty-nine and she, good god, is sixty-one. There was a time long ago, when he was just out of college and her husband and son had moved to Mexico, when they might have become lovers, she remembers certain nervous sharp looks he gave her, but the looks were always accompanied by a manner so aloof that it repelled all possible advances, which in any case she wouldn't have allowed herself to make to a boy who might as well have been her own son. Still, she wonders whether she made a mistake back then, in that time of early friendship, when he so clearly needed to be rescued from something, poor kid, with his nervous sharp looks and his torrent of words, though of course she hadn't wanted to *get in his way*, she hadn't wanted to be *that kind of woman*. But then he had shut himself up in the house with his mother, he had moved into the attic room and begun keeping peculiar hours. And she had moved to cheaper quarters out by the GE plant at the edge of town, renting a two-floor apartment in a brick row house. Twice a week he would visit her with his looks and his talk, and always a question seemed to hang in the air between them. That was a long time ago, and still he hadn't finished his book, he would never finish, though maybe one day, who could tell. And should she have said, fifteen years ago, laying her hand on his arm: please stay the night?—she *the older woman*, the *woman of experience*. She has never spoken to him of her lovers, only of her jobs. He doesn't understand very much about the world, her Haverstraw. She wonders whether she should have said to him, back then, laying her fingers on his forearm: come upstairs, why don't you. It's hot under the lamp bulb. Through the screens she can hear the sound of insects, crickets are they—the sound of summer.

SONG OF THE FIELD INSECTS

Red rover, red rover
The summer's over
Chk-a-chk mmmm.
By and by
Chk-a-chk mmmm
You too shall die
Chk-a-chk mmmm
Chk-a-chk mmmm

THREE YOUNG MEN

Three young men stand in the moon-speckled shadow of a copper beech in the corner of the library parking lot. Light from a lantern on a post shines on the recently tarred pavement, which glimmers with a satiny black sheen. The young men stand out of the light, in leaf shadow that isn't thick enough to keep out the moonlight. The tallest speaks, quietly and urgently.

"Here's the deal. I walk across the lot to the door. Just out for a little walk minding my own sweet business. I open her up and go in. That's all there is to it so listen to me. You don't move and you don't talk and you stay back here out of sight. Once I get in there I'll let you know."

"Where's the key? You got the key?"

"Key's right here. Don't sweat the key."

"We have to go across the lot?"

"You go straight across the lot. You're not doing anything wrong, right? so you don't look like you're doing anything wrong. Just out for a little stroll, officer. Hey, smile: you're on *Candid Camera.*"

"Anybody sees us, we're dead."

"Anybody sees you, you're dead. Anybody sees me, I'm cool. But who's awake, man? It's one o'clock in the fucking morning. Just watch for cop cars and play dead. When I'm in there I'll let you know. Like so. Then you walk. You don't run. You walk. Piece of cake."

Smitty walks briskly across the bright parking lot, looking straight ahead, to the dark green door at the side of the library. He opens a fist, revealing a brass key that glints in the yellow light from the bare bulb over the door. He inserts the key, turns, and pushes his way in. From the shadows he motions to Blake and Danny. They hesitate, begin to walk into the glow of the lamppost, stop in confusion. Danny breaks into a run. Blake walks fast, looking left and right.

"Real pretty, real professional," Smitty says, shutting the door behind them. It is so dark they can't see each other.

"Now what," Danny says.

THE WOMAN WHO LIVES ALONE

I am the woman who lives alone. I have no husband, no children, no lover, not even a cat. Please do not think I mind living alone, in my old house, among my things. But on such a night, when the moon is a white blossom in a blue garden, it is good to walk outside in the back yard, and to breathe deep among the zinnias. You who lack the courage to live alone, do not dare to pity me. Only sometimes, on such a night, I would like to hear the sound of voices. We who live alone can grow funny in our habits, because there are no others to tell us about ourselves. Sometimes we put on only one sock. Sometimes we speak aloud, in the warm night air. How good it is, on such a night, to walk about in the yard, to smell the freshness of the grass. Surely there is no law against it.

THE MOON
AND THE MANNEQUIN

The moon, climbing so slowly that no one notices, shines down on Main Street. It casts a deep shadow on one side of the street and an eerie brightness on the other, where the sidewalk is bone-white and the little glass windows of the parking meters glisten as if they are wet. In the store windows you can see far back. Moonlight shines on jars of olives and loaves of hardcrusted bread in the window of the Italian grocery. It shines on rows of eyeglass frames that cast long, sharp shadows on the optometrist's wall, it shines on the brilliant white towel on the back of the barber's chair and the glass bottles reflected in the glimmer of the barber's mirror. It shines on the breakfast table with its four empty cereal bowls patterned with apples, on the folded shirts and striped neckties, on the white sandals of the mannequin in the department-store window. Moonlight lies on her cheeks, on her long fingers and half-parted lips. She feels the moonlight penetrating her fiberglass skin, soothing her, lulling her will; she feels a swooning languor combined with a secret excitement, a loosening of the rigorous bonds of her nature. Under the rays of moonlight, her hidden life is awaking. There is a tremor in her fingers; one hand bends slightly at the wrist. Behind her sunglasses, slowly her eyelids close and open.

THE CHILDREN WAKE

In rooms with windows looking out at moonlit yards, in beds with covers picturing bears and ballerinas, the children begin to wake. Through the summer screens they hear dim music rising slowly and slowly falling, a dim and distant music, calling. What is that dim music? The children push the covers back, swing their legs quickly over the bedside. Their eyes are alert, their heads tipped slightly to one side, on the smooth skin between their eyebrows faint lines of concentration appear.

STILLNESS

Janet's yard is absolutely still. It looks to her like a painting of a yard at night: BACK YARD: SUMMER NIGHT. Or maybe it's called GIRL IN WINDOW, WAITING. Only an idiot would stay kneeling at a window on a summer night, waiting, and for what?—not that there's anything better to do. She wonders if she's visible from down there. The yard is bordered on the right by a tall hedge that can be trimmed only if you stand on a stepladder. At the bottom the stems are thick, like tree branches, with spaces to crawl through. To the left is the garage, the long side in shadow, the front white-brilliant in moonlight. The back of the yard is bordered by a stand of evergreens, spruce and a few Scotch pines, behind which a wire fence separates the yard from the next yard. And after that: another yard. Yard after yard, little rectangles, stretching to the end of town, stretching all the way across America. Maybe you could duck through hedges, climb fences, pass sandboxes and baseball bats, and one day, pushing through the last hedge, suddenly—violins, please!—the Pacific. And all the lovely summer life of yards: kids playing tag, badminton nets, barbecues, people lounging around in aluminum folding chairs, beach towels drying on the porch rail, night voices drifting up to your window. But now the yard is still—asleep—bound in a spell. In front of the trees, not quite belonging to them, is the big old silver maple, tall and thick-trunked. From one high branch hangs a rope swing. Most of the wooden seat is in shadow, but an edge catches the moonlight. But the swing can never swing, and the girl in the window can never turn her head, because they're both trapped in the painting. Everything is motionless, so motionless that it seems to Janet that motion is being held back, as if the yard has taken a deep breath and is trying not to let it out—at any moment an accident will happen, a tell-tale movement will take place. Or maybe the yard is filling up with stillness, a stillness that will become greater and greater till finally it brims over. At the window Janet waits, afraid to move.

THE MAN WITH GREEN EYES

William Cooper, twenty-eight years old, known as Coop to the guys at Big Mama's, sets his beer glass carefully down in the exact center of the scallop-edged paper napkin, rises unsteadily from the red leatherette seat in the booth, and raises his fingertips to his temple in a salute that takes in the bartender, the guys in the booth, the crowded tables, the brown and red and green bottles reflected in the mirror behind the bar, the pewter steins hanging from hooks, before he turns on his heel and makes his way out to the street. The air is warm, almost hot, but with a touch of coolness wrapped up in the warmth, and the strangeness of it strikes him: the night air warm and cool, the sky dark and bright—there's a thought there somewhere, if only he can stop things from turning. Coop passes the lit-up window of Curtis's Electric Supply, where he glances at the porcelain table lamps with pink shades, the glass-paneled lanterns with black-enameled frames, the neat packages of wall switches and socket mounts. At the drugstore he looks at the far lightbulb shining on the pharmacy counter, sort of pretty back there, before he pauses at the cardboard cutout of a blue-eyed blonde in a white bikini. She's always there, night after night, holding up a bottle of soda covered with big drops of moisture. Her teeth are whiter than the bathing suit, her tanned shoulders are glossy as new baseball bats. Her breasts, the size of kickballs, seem to be smiling too. She's friendly, available, everybody's favorite girl, high school cheerleader in cute white skirt, life of the party, a million laughs, Miss Popularity, a real knockout, man is she built, get a load a that, check her out, but Coop is disdainful. She is nothing compared to the lady he loves, the high-class lady who doesn't offer herself to every passerby but holds herself cool and aloof, out of reach, a little high-and-mighty maybe but that's all right, a woman has to protect herself. In the window he sees his own dim reflection staring: coppery hair, green eyes, red-cracked whites. He looks quickly away and sees himself looking quickly away. Guilty, yer honor. Coop crosses a side street, glances down it at the power lines above the railroad tracks, and continues along the sidewalk on Main. He passes the window of volleyballs and basketballs, the window of pens and leather notebooks, the window bathed in cool blue light showing a poster of a tropical island with a palm tree, a flamingo, and a woman in an orange bathing suit lying on her stomach on white sand with one leg raised at the knee. Now that's more like it, Coop thinks: a woman alone, a woman with secrets. But he's getting closer, already he's crossing another street. The blue mailbox shining in the light of the corner streetlamp makes him think of a gigantic moneybank. As a kid he had a tin moneybank shaped like a mailbox, never saved more than a dollar. Story of his life. He passes the barber shop and the Italian grocery with its basket of twisted bread. As he comes to the first window of the department store, with its breakfast table set for four, he takes a deep breath, trying to calm himself.

HAVERSTRAW SPEAKS

Haverstraw sits on the worn maroon couch with its faint shine on the curve of the right arm. Beside him on the lamp table a glass of ice water rests on a cork-bottomed coaster with a white-tiled top picturing a blue Yankee clipper. Beside the glass is a cereal bowl filled with pretzel sticks. Across from him, on the brown armchair, Mrs. Kasco sits with her legs tucked up, her fuzzy red slippers lying on the rug. She holds a cigarette in her right hand and a glass of red wine in the left. On the table beside her are a lamp, a green glass ashtray shaped like a leaf with a stem, and two books: an old hardback copy of *Jennie Gerhardt* with a faded title, and a fat library book called *The Arms of Krupp*. A rattling floor fan blows directly at her, stirring her kimono and fluttering the blue smoke that drifts to the ceiling. Through the trembling smoke Haverstraw sees the stairway banister and the old bookcase in which he can make out a broken-spined Modern Library Giant edition of *Studs Lonigan* and two volumes of *The Decline of the West*. On top of the bookcase, cutting into the line of the balusters, an Unabridged Webster's, Second Edition, lies open, one side higher than the other. A red eyeglass case rests in the valley where the pages meet. Mrs. Kasco's brown, intelligent, slightly prominent eyes behind her blue-framed glasses are watching him intently as he speaks.

"What bothers me I guess is the lie of it all, I mean the inevitable lie of the form itself, since the second you say 'I' you're immediately separating yourself from the person you're claiming yourself to be, am I making myself clear, so that the 'I' which is supposed to be the sign of authenticity is really the most devious pronoun of all, nothing but a 'he' in disguise, a 'he' with false beard and mustache. Because when you say 'I' you're no longer the 'I' you claim to be, but someone else, a stranger spied on by your present self, separate, severed, estranged. Am I making myself clear? *I sat down.* What can it mean except *The stranger sat down,* the one I once was but no longer am? And so I protest against the false intimacy, the pretense that this alien 'I,' this stranger, is putting you right there, at the moment of the act. But even aside from that, aside from that, there's the worse problem of reporting anything with even a shred of accuracy, a shred. Hopeless. Because the slightest act, the lifting of my left pinkie, is accompanied by a thousand thoughts and sensations, which surround it like a, like a, hell I don't know, a halo, or no, say a suffusion, an emanation, and without these sensations you're writing abstractions, generalizations, do you know what I…Take nouns. Every noun names a class. It's a summary, a blur. But my bed, my chair, my window, these are as precise as my whole life, do you follow me. And so it's hard, I keep losing the thread, what with the lie of the 'I' and the lie of the noun, the awful simplifications that pass themselves off as memory. Memory! What do they mean by memory, anyway? That passage I read you by what's-his-name, remember? about the araucarias. You look at the araucarias, all the intricacies of their leaves and branches are impressed on your retina, you *see* them with absolute authority, but the next day a slight blurring is noticeable, in a week you remember the trees but without that intensity of exactness, and in a year? Ten years? And that's true of all memory. So what is memory after all but an act of forgetting, of omission. And so there's nothing but loss, falling away, carelessness, oblivion. Lies, all lies."

"Well, but hold your horses here. Aren't you leaving something out?"

"Oh sure, sure, you mean my debt to society and all that dead Marxist crap."

"You could do a hell of a lot worse than read a little Marx, my friend. It wouldn't hurt you one little bit to think about class, about class values."

"All I ask of society is to let me paddle my own canoe."

"Right. Perfect. And who do you think rents you the canoe? Who gives you permission to use the stream? Where does the money come from that lets you do your paddling? But listen, I meant something else. You were speaking about memory."

"I don't remember. That's a joke, by the way."

"You said there's nothing but forgetting. But what about those little sharp memories, we all have them. I forget say a whole summer, but I remember one teacup—the chip near the handle, the tea stains along the rim. So it's not true, exactly, what you say."

"But don't you see how that just exactly supports what I've been killing myself trying to say? You admit the blur, the loss, a whole summer gone, I mean you might as well not've lived at all, good-bye cruel world!—and up rises one lousy teacup, one pathetic little crummy teacup, which only by contrast seems a miracle of precision. But in itself it's—it's nothing, a rough sketch, a blur, you don't see it at all, not in anything like its full marvelous detail, it's just a few broken bits washed up on shore after a shipwreck. Or it's like one of those characters in Dickens. You know: red nose, stiff collar, chalky shirtcuff. Nothing but that. All the rest invisible."

"But you see that character. You fill him in."

"But that's the point! You fill him in. You fill him in with your imagination. That's just exactly the godforsaken point. You fill him in. Memory keeps turning into imagination. The world—the fact—the actual—keeps slipping away. Memory is impossible. The whole enterprise is doomed."

"And you really believe that? That it's hopeless?"

"Yes. No. I don't know."

CHORUS OF NIGHT VOICES

Come out, come out, wherever you are, you dreamers and drown-
ers, you loafers and losers, you shadow-seekers and orphans of the
sun. Come out, come out, you flops and fizzlers, you good-for-
nothings and down-and-outers, day's outcasts, dark's little darlin's.
Come on, all you who are misbegotten and woebegone, all you
with black thoughts and red fever-visions, come on, you small-
town Ishmaels with your sad blue eyes, you plain Janes and hard-
luck guys, come, you gripers and groaners, you goners and loners,
you sadsacks and shlemiels, come on, come on, you pale romantics
and pie-eyed Palookas, you has-beens and never-will-bes, you sun-
mocked and day-doomed denizens of the dark: come out into the
night.

THE DOLLS WAKE

In the attics of the town, the dolls begin to wake. These are not dolls in the freshness of their youth, the dolls who dwell in children's bedrooms, but old, abandoned dolls, no longer believed in. They lean back against boxes of old dishes, sit slumped on broken-backed chairs, lie face down on attic floorboards. Unremembered, unimagined, unenlivened by the attention of their owners, they lie drained and empty, stiff as dead flowers. But on this summer night, when the almost full moon wakens sleepers in their beds, the dolls in their long slumber begin to stir. The cloth doll with yellow yarn hair and painted blue eyes sits up and smooths her rumpled apron. The one-eyed cuddly bear looks about. The dusty elephant raises his trunk, the Dutch doll with hard-lashed eyes glances toward Little Boy Blue, Columbine flutters her eyelashes and turns away from Pierrot, who sorrowfully bows his flour-pale head, while in the puppet theater the hook-nosed man with very black eyebrows and a very sharp chin stares at the girl with blond braids and a turned-up nose, who steals a glance at the blue-eyed drummer boy stirring in his sleep and dreaming of a high tower, a forest of thorns, a princess slowly opening her eyes.

THE SWING

The world, filled to the brim with stillness, suddenly overflows: a
hedge branch moves, through the hedge a hand appears, and then
he's there, in the yard, glancing up at the windows with his hair
falling over his forehead. Janet feels a pain of happiness, a swooning terrible pain that is like grief. She has never felt anything like
this knife-twist of happiness, this dark joy that seizes her like suf-
fering. He can't see her in the dark window, and she is glad: she
imagines her face to be desolate with love. He walks through
bright moonlight into the shade of the silver maple, and his grace-
ful walk across the yard is like a wind she feels on her skin. He sits
down on the swing. He hooks his arms around the ropes. Frowns
up at her window, scuffs a sandal on the patch of dirt. The bent
ropes, the turn of his neck, his anklebone above the sandal, all this
seems as mysterious and beautiful as the moonlight pouring into
the yard. Then he pushes off and begins to swing. He is pulling
back on the ropes, he is reaching his legs out, stretching, swinging
into the light of the moon. Then back, his legs bending as he
swings into shade. Light, dark, light, dark, his loose pants rippling
as he swings. And the swinging releases her: she waves, she laughs,
but his attention is fiercely concentrated on his swinging, for him
there is nothing but that. Oh why is he swinging on her swing like
that, forgetting her, annihilating her? Janet turns from the window,
throws her leather jacket over her nightgown, hurries barefoot
down the thickly carpeted stairs.

IN THE LIBRARY

The darkness on the second floor is cut by streaks of yellow light from the streetlamps on Main Street. Through the high, arched windows the dark blue night-sky is suffused with moonglow. In the lounge Blake and Danny sit in leather armchairs that are half-turned toward a leather couch, where Smitty lies with his head resting on a couch-arm. An ashtray with a burning cigarette rests on his stomach. With one hand he supports a bottle of beer on his chest.

"Go on," Blake says.

"So I'm sitting there on the couch like a good little Boy Scout with one hand hanging down over her shoulder accidentally on purpose with my fingers sort of touching her tit through her blouse which is made of this very silky material and I'm thinking what is the best way to advance the action without blowing my cool."

"Go on," Blake says.

"So I start kissing her and she's kissing me back like she might be interested in male Caucasians but please don't jump to any con-clusions and my other hand just happens to be resting on her knee which when I look down I see her skirt is pushed up and I'm look-ing at all of it, man. I mean this girl is giving me the *view* all the way up the aven*ue*. So I start moving my hand real slow and easy up the old leg like I'm a cat burglar crawling across a roof and either she doesn't notice or she don't care."

"Her mind is on higher things," Blake says.

"So that's the downtown action and meantime uptown back at the ranch I've got my hand on this button on her blouse and I'm sort of fiddling with it and hey, how about that, it slips through the buttonhole, just one of those things."

"A little accident," Blake says.

"I'm innocent as a baby in a cradle saying googoo."

"You're innocent and I'm the Virgin Mary," Blake says.

"So down in the valley, valley so low, I'm working my way up an inch at a time and meanwhile on top of old Smokey all covered with snow I've got my hand under her blouse and I'm feeling her up through her bra which has these fancy lacy edges, man. She doesn't stop me and I'm starting to ask myself how far I can go."

"You'll go far, young man," Blake says.

"So I'm sitting there hard at work on the late-night shift with one hand jammed up against the front of her panties and the other hand shoved up under her bra and her just sitting there letting me feel everything which is making me very curious about just what else is going to take place with this chick whose acquaintance I am making."

"He was always a curious student, interested in his studies," Blake says.

"So I've got one hand down in Cherry Lane and the other up in Jug Alley and tell you the truth I'm getting a little tired of doing the cha cha cha when it's time to start jumpin' to a rock-roll beat. She's sitting there with her blouse hanging down over her belt buckle and her bombs swinging in the breeze and her skirt up around her elbows and the way I figure it the time has come for every good man to come to the aid of his country."

"The Army Wants *You*," Blake says.

"I consider the situation and decide the best way for me to go in the situation which is looking good from where I sit is to take it slow and go with the flow. Stay loose as a goose and then vamoose. So before she knows what hits her I bend over and kiss her very sweet and polite like I am not making out with a cunt on a couch but I'm her long-lost brother come back from the orphanage. This is definitely the way to go because she's hot to trot and hey why not. So I'm sitting there kissing her all brotherly sisterly and one of those things just happens to happen which is that I just happen to stick my tongue in her mouth. You will fucking not believe what happens next."

"What happens next," Blake says.

"What happens next is she sits up and pushes me away and yanks down her skirt like she just noticed she's not alone in her wigwam down on the reservation. 'Fresh!' she says. I fucking swear to God that's what she says. She's so pissed she looks like she's about to spit blood. Can you believe it? One hand halfway up her fallopian tubes and one hand buried in her bazooms and it's good clean all-American fun but one false move with the old tongue and she wants to stick me on a banana boat and ship me back to Brazil. I fucking couldn't believe it, man. Can you believe it?"

"I can't believe it," Blake says, crestfallen.

"Dumb bitch," Smitty says.

Danny stands up and walks to a window. He looks down at the bank, at the store windows on Main Street, at a stoplight changing from red to green. Up above, the sky is a dark, radiant blue. He feels a sudden desire: to smash through the glass, to float up into that blue radiance.

THE MAN WITH
SHINY BLACK HAIR

Out for a stroll on this fine summer night, the man with shiny black hair passes the library. Blue-dark the arched windows in moonlight: a nice effect. Panes throwing back tree branches and the corner lamppost. The man with shiny black hair imagines the moonlit aisles, where earlier in the day he gathered pictures for his gallery. That was before the blond man in the trenchcoat made him nervous. The lights of Main Street, even at 1:34 in the morning, make him nervous. The little yellow lights on the movie marquee seem to be going round and round, round and round, an infuriating illusion. He needs calm, darkness, calm. Quickly he crosses Main Street and heads over the iron bridge above the railroad tracks. Glitter of rails, black towers in the sky, the mass of overhead wires stretching away. He'll walk around awhile, up past the high school, out of harm's way, who knows what he'll find, maybe another picture for his collection, you never can tell.

THE PLEASURES OF
WINDOW GAZING

Coop stops unsteadily before the window where the tall and lovely lady stands higher than the street. She looks down at the world through sunglasses darker than the night. Her nose is so thin that each nostril is no wider than a pencil line. Her legs are so long that each one seems an entire tall woman. Under the soft material of her peach-colored dress her small breasts, high and round, look as hard as billiard balls. Her long smooth fingers are slightly bent, as if they're holding an invisible, delicate object. For some reason all this makes Coop think of marble fountains and cool water. As he looks up at her, a sudden longing ripples over him, as if someone has drawn a fingernail across the skin of his stomach. And his heart is moved, though his hands feel thick and clumsy by his sides. His nails are black with engine grease. He isn't worthy of touching the strap of her sandal. He feels sunk in his worthlessness, a drunk on his way home, but then again it's a free country, anyone can look, so why not him? The street is trembling, the air is trembling. The lady herself seems none too steady on her pins. As he tries to concentrate his attention, he sees a little tremor in her finger. In her dark glasses the stoplight changes from red to green, there's a glow of green on her bare shoulder, the lady is trembling and shimmering, Coop feels a tug in his stomach, and stepping forward until he's next to the window, he closes his eyes, rises a little on his toes, and, pushing out his lips, places on the cool glass a heartfelt kiss.

THE BEACH ON A
SUMMER NIGHT

On this warm night in August, at this late hour—it's 1:42 in the morning—the beach is quiet but not deserted. For this is the hour of lovers and loners, who come down to the water long after the others have left. The lovers lie in each other's arms on old army blankets, or on towels placed side by side. Sometimes they lie down in full moonlight. Sometimes they seek the shadows cast by the three lifeguard chairs, or the upside-down rowboat, or the side of the closed refreshment stand. The loners sit looking out at the water, or walk along the shore. One sits high up on a lifeguard chair, staring out at the dark-bright water of the Sound; another sits on a rock at the end of the jetty, smoking a cigarette; a third walks along the hard wet sand, shiny in the moonlight, between the crooked line of seaweed and the water's edge. On this night the waves are very small. They break slowly and quietly, unrolling along the wet sand in orderly lines that suddenly are broken by new lines, in a pattern difficult to grasp. The loners, as they watch the unrolling of the waves, are careful to avoid each other. They are even more careful to avoid the lovers, who seem to feel they have a right to the whole beach. The lovers, for their part, take pains to avoid other lovers and are irked by the presence of the loners, whose footsteps sometimes pass so close to a blanket that the lovers grow tense. The lovers and loners are therefore very much aware of each other, but it is difficult to know what they are thinking. Are the lovers grateful to the loners for making them feel fortunate? Do they perhaps envy the loners their night freedom, far from the demands and desires of another creature? As for the loners, it's easy to imagine that they are irritated by the lovers, who remind them of their loneliness, and who invade the beach as if to take over the last preserve of the solitary wanderer. It's possible of course that the loners, for reasons obscure to them, have come to the beach precisely because they know that the lovers will be here, on this warm summer night. The tide is going out. Small dark sandbars glisten like wet glass. On the licorice-dark water a bar of moonlight stretches from a point just beyond the low-breaking waves to a point just short of the horizon. The bar is solid in places, as if painted carefully with a brush, but in other places it is shaky, and here and there it breaks into quivering points of light. Far out on the water, a white light appears on top of a black lighthouse and goes out. It will not return for another five seconds. Downshore, on a far point of land where a roller coaster used to stand, a small red light flashes once a second on top of a radio tower. In the distance the green and red lights of channel markers blink on and off. At the horizon, where the radiant dark-blue sky is distinct from the black water, you can make out a narrow strip of land: the dark hills of Long Island. The moon is large and paper-white, with blue shadows.

SECRETS

Janet runs barefoot across the lawn turned gem-green by the moon, a fairytale green, the green of lost cities at the bottoms of lakes in the depths of dark forests, she is running across the bottom of a green lake but something is wrong and she hesitates as she nears the swing. He doesn't turn, doesn't look at her, just sits staring the other way, how is it possible, he doesn't love her at all, god what a fool she's been, all alone now under the blue sky of the dead summer night. He turns, he smiles, ah the charmer, the heartbreaker—rises to meet her. She flings herself into his hug, because what else is there to do really, and besides she's a little crazy on this night, oh she's moon-mad, summer-loony, and anyway who cares, not her. He spins her around, lifts her into the air, sweeps her off her feet, her handsome one, her lovely one. She can't bear this happiness hurting her like pain. Now he stands back, gives a little bow—a bow!—sweeps out his hand: he is offering her the swing. For you, my dear. Sir, you are too kind. And she sits, and she begins to swing, reaching out her legs, leaning way back, rippling into moonlight and back into leafshade, while he pushes gently-hard, his hands firm against her hips in the summer nightgown. Then he stands aside and allows her to swing by herself. She ripples into moonlight, her nightgown fluttering, her tanned legs shining under the moon—she swings with flung-back face, looking at him upside down, laughing suddenly into the moon-mad sky. And at the top of her arc, watch me now, she lets go: for a moment she seems suspended in the moon-heavy air, lying lazily back, a girl stretched out on moonlight, but she feels the breeze on her face, the tug of the earth, and she's down, panting, laughing.

"You're wild tonight," he says laughing: approving.

"Think so?" she says, throwing back her hair, lifting her face to the moon.

"When I was a kid," she continues, "I had a hideout, right over there. My secret place."

She leads him into the spruces. The needles are soft and sharp on her bare feet, cool and crackly. Against her hands the prickly twigs feel like many hairbrushes. She ducks her head, fights her way in, laughs, sits, feels him sit next to her. Shaded by thick branches, they look out at the swing and the moonlit yard.

"I like secrets," she says. "Don't you?"

THE CHILDREN SET FORTH

The children are opening the doors of their bedrooms, they are passing through rooms touched by moonlight. There is moonlight on the rug with the green parrots, moonlight on the kitchen clock shaped like a teapot, moonlight on the arm of the mahogany rocker and on the porcelain milkmaid with the little pail on the mantelpiece. The children open the doors of their houses softly and step out into the warm summer night. They can hear the cry of the insects, the sound of the trucks on the thruway, and far away a faint music, rising and falling, dark and sweet, restless as dreams, lovelier than sleep, music unending.

BLACK MASKS

On the top step of the long wraparound porch, cluttered with flow-erpots and old furniture, a tall shadow appears. The side of the porch is fierce with moonlight and sharp black shade, but here the porch is nearly dark, except for the thin light of a distant streetlamp partly concealed by a Norway maple. The tall shadow glides to a front window and pushes up against the screen, which rattles but does not move. At a second window the buckled screen jiggles in its track. Slowly, jerkily, it rises, grating, squeaking. Behind the screen the wood-framed window, rain-swollen, scrapes upward with repeated palm-thrusts. Now the shadow slips through the opening and into the dark house, now the front door opens inward, the wooden screen door is unlatched. Four girls wearing black masks rise from the bushes.

In the musty parlor, smelling of old rugs and furniture polish, they sit on sag-cushioned chairs with doilies on the arms and a too-soft squeaky couch. Summer Storm ranges silently, open-ing table drawers and little boxes. A streak of moonlight on a wall catches a small oval mirror, illuminates a patch of wallpaper showing a barefoot boy rolling a hoop. On the couchback a doll sits with wide-open eyes and a little rosebud mouth. Summer Storm stops, listens, and sends Black Star, her second in command, into the next room. The house is quiet, except for the faint sounds of Black Star moving about. She returns and raises both arms, crossed at the wrists: the all-clear sign. Summer Storm finds in the drawer of a lamp table an old mousetrap, which she shows to each member of the gang in turn, before handing it over to Night Rider, who writes the note: WE ARE YOUR DAUGHTERS. A fourth member is dispatched to the kitchen and returns with a box of stale crackers and a screw-top jar of much too tart apple juice. The masked girls settle back on their cushions, while Summer Storm sits Indian-style on the floor, straight-backed, hands on knees, alert, listening.

LAURA FOLLOWS THE MOON

Laura has wandered away from the lamplit streets of her ranch-house neighborhood, but at the back of the Congregational Church she feels visible from the dark second-floor windows of a nearby house with gables and a tower. Where can she go? Where? Behind the elementary school the long shadows of swing-posts stretch sharply across the pale bright sand. The sand reminds her of a beach. Where on earth? Where? Her legs are growing tired. The town is too spread out, you could walk for days. You could walk for days all night. Down to the library, across Main, over the iron bridge above the railroad tracks, past the long steps and fat beach-colored pillars of the high school. Why did the moron bring a ladder to school? Because he wanted to be in high school. Shelter is what she needs, shelter, but in the parking lot behind the high school two bright lights shine on the asphalt stretching away, put a gleam on a solitary black car with a long shadow. In the wire fence of the empty tennis courts, a green tennis ball is stuck in the mesh high up. Her legs are killing her. She thinks she must have been walking for an hour, for hours, impossible to tell, nothing changes in the night. The whole town is beginning to feel like her room. She's got to get out of here, got to find something, and when she looks up at the sky she knows that the moon will take her where she needs to go.

CON AMOR DE LA MUERTE

"I think what I need," Haverstraw says, "what I would really like, at this moment of my life, at this point in the late twentieth century, is a breath of fresh air. Come with me? Just across the street, I mean. It can't be much past two."

"Just let me throw on a sweater over this damn thing."

Across the street from the row of attached brick houses runs a sidewalk lit by a single streetlamp. Behind the sidewalk lies a strip of grass with a slatted wooden bench, and behind the bench rises a slope broken by a rocky outcrop and topped by a few oaks and pines. Haverstraw, chewing a pretzel, and Mrs. Kasco, smoking a cigarette and carrying in one hand a glass of wine, pass under the streetlamp and pause at the bench. Mrs. Kasco glances at Haverstraw, who steps up to the slope and begins to climb, turning to offer her his hand. She is wearing high heels. From the wide rock ledges grow tufts of high grass and gigantic dandelions with flowers the size of silver dollars. At the first ledge Mrs. Kasco takes off her heels and carries them in her right hand, pinched between thumb and two fingers. She leaves her cigarette in her mouth as she offers first the wineglass and then her other hand to Haverstraw and climbs up to the second ledge.

"An adventure," she says laughing.

"I didn't mean to ruin your feet."

"I don't know why I put on these things. They were just there, by the door."

At the top he looks around quickly at the tree roots and dead leaves and pine needles. On the other side of the slope he can see a moonlit vacant lot littered with old tires among patches of goldenrod. The lot peters out at the back of a gas station. Haverstraw takes off his nylon windbreaker and lays it on the ground, before a tree trunk, and with a little bow he sweeps out his arm.

"Well, I don't see why not," Mrs. Kasco says, and sits down with her back against the trunk, facing the brick apartments.

"Not a bad view, really," Haverstraw says as he hands her the glass of wine. He sits down on the ground beside her and draws up his long legs, slightly spread. He embraces his knees with his arms, grasping his left wrist in his right hand.

"Care for a nightcap?" Mrs. Kasco says. She holds out the glass of wine.

"No. Sure, why not."

Haverstraw takes a drink and hands back the glass. A car passes on the street below them.

"A few nights ago," Haverstraw says, "I was driving on the thruway, around two in the morning, just driving along you understand, and a car comes up on my right, low-slung, skirts, a meanlooking hunk of tin. Four guys in it, tough, young, out of the project. I remember hoping they wouldn't kill me, but they weren't even looking my way. But what struck me was what they'd painted on the side of the car. In big letters, very neat: CON AMOR DE LA MUERTE."

"You shouldn't drive around up there at night like that."

"But I mean, think of painting those words on the side of your car. Talk about street poetry. Poets of death. I felt like bowing my head out of sheer respect. Bowing my head."

"Here's a piece of advice from a wise old woman. Never bow your head when you're driving on the thruway at two in the morning. Here's another piece of advice. Never bow your head at all."

Haverstraw looks out at the empty street with its patch of shine from the streetlamp, at the dark apartments with bare bulbs over the front doors, at the dark blue sky faintly orange at the bottom from a strip of diners and gas stations a few blocks away.

"It's good out here," he says. "I can breathe now."

"The forest primeval, or what the corporations have left us of it. This is the forest primeval. The murmuring pines and the hemlocks. I had to memorize fifty lines of that thing in the eighth grade. But I'll tell you what. I could do without that smell."

"What is it?"

"It's from the brakelining plant over on South Broad."

"Well, I don't care. I don't ask for much. Even Sherwood Forest probably had beer cans all over the place. Miller. Bud. Think of Friar Tuck. All those six-packs."

"Look up there. Look. See it?"

Through a tangle of black leaves and branches, high overhead, Haverstraw sees the bright white moon. It's so bright he has to look away.

"Isn't it lovely," Mrs. Kasco says.

"To me it looks like a flashy ad. An ad for eternity. Buy one, get one free."

"I hate that. I goddam hate it when you do that."

"Oh, hell. I didn't mean anything by it."

"Things will work out," Mrs. Kasco says, resting her fingers lightly on his forearm.

Wearily Haverstraw bows his head onto his raised knees.

THE WHITE FLOWER

In moonlit attics filled with cast-off things, the dolls are moving about. The cloth doll with yellow yarn hair picks up a marble and puts it in her apron pocket, the drummer boy walks back and forth through a sliver of moonlight that turns the arm of his jacket a brilliant blue, the one-eyed cuddly bear walks around an old toybox into a shadowy place where he sees a pair of old boxing gloves, an upside-down sled with rusty runners, a towering chest of drawers. As he rounds a corner of the chest of drawers, he sees a white, billowy arm holding out a white flower. The one-eyed cuddly bear stops uncertainly. He sees it is the arm of Pierrot, in his loose white tunic with the billowy sleeves. Pierrot is kneeling and holding out the flower to Columbine, who already is walking away with a pert toss of her head. The one-eyed cuddly bear watches as the flower drops to the floor without a sound. His one eye is round with wonder. The thin white hand, at the end of the low-hanging sleeve, remains outstretched.

DANNY ALONE

Danny turns from the window and walks over to the leather couch on which Smitty is lying with the glass ashtray on his stomach. The ashtray rises and falls gently as he breathes. Behind the couch Danny rests one hand lightly on the couchback.

"I'm going."

"The hell you are," Blake says.

"Let him go," Smitty says.

"What's wrong," Blake says.

"Nothing. I need to walk."

"He needs to fucking walk," Blake says.

"Don't start anything," Smitty says. "Just don't start anything."

"I'm not starting anything. Danny wants to walk, he can walk. It's a free fucking country."

"Right."

"Only I'm thinking maybe Danny doesn't like pussy. You like pussy, Danny?"

"I said don't start anything," Smitty says, sitting up. The ashtray falls to the rug.

"I'm not starting anything."

"Careful when you leave, Danny. We don't want trouble."

"If anybody sees you," Blake says, outraged.

Down the stairs, through the door, across the bright-lit parking lot into the shadows of the trees. Danny moves between the row of trees and a few parked cars to the side street, turns right and passes the front of the library, crosses Main Street and heads for home. He likes Smitty, who admires him and protects him, but Blake is always flaring up, jealous, furious, waiting to strike a blow. It's hard for Danny to remember how he fell in with Smitty; he's definitely out of his element. Suddenly he's stealing keys from the drawer in the library, breaking in. Proving something. Showoff. Bigshot. Look, Ma, no hands. He isn't even sure what Smitty sees in him. Sometimes it makes him uneasy, as if he's got something Smitty wants: good grades, friendships with smart girls, a serious witty father and laughing smart mother. Smitty once came over after school and talked for an hour with his mother, very serious, his language careful, formal, his face creased with thought. Smitty has brains, but he always has to put on a little act: tough guy act, good guy act, cool act. Sometimes Danny is bored by Smitty, deeply bored, but he doesn't want to think about that now. He is sixteen years old and has never kissed a girl, never touched a girl—it drives him crazy and he doesn't know what to do about it. If any girl sat next to him on a couch and let him touch her body he knows exactly what he would feel: a gratitude so deep that it would be deeper than love. The night is warm, with a little ripple of coolness in it. He passes over the bridge above the railroad tracks and looks down at the tracks stretching away toward New York and at the black crisscross structures across the tracks; he wonders what they're called. He's got to get that key back. He walks on, past the railroad parking lot, past the dark high school, under the thruway overpass, mostly trucks at this hour. Maybe he'll chuck college and take to the highways, a truck driver with an elbow out the window, crossing the country at night, silent and alone. The sudden brightness of all-night diners, the steaming coffee in thick white cups as heavy as rocks. Diana Santangelo laughs at his jokes and sometimes touches him on the forearm when she laughs. When she laughs her shoulders shake, her silky blouse shakes, her hair shakes, and she hugs her books so tightly to her chest that they seem to be pressing painfully into her breasts. He tries to imagine what it would be like to have breasts: big jiggly shaky things stuck up there for everyone to see, big bobbly bouncers. Jumpy jouncy jigglers. Better to be a guy, stuff it out of sight. Girls in skirts and blouses, girls in summer dresses. To be in the cab of an eighteen-wheeler, alone, on the highways of the night.

Tired now: great peaceful waves of it, shuddering up his arms.

SKINTIGHT

The man with shiny black hair stands in shadow at the back of the high school and watches the girl in skintight jeans walk across the empty bright parking lot. There is a lost look about her, the look of a waif, a suburban gamine. Perhaps she's in need of a friend. I'll be *your* friend if you'll be *my* friend. It is not good for a girl in skintight jeans to walk the streets alone at night: no no no no: someone should inform her mother. Her hair swings like a horsetail at the small of her back, switch switch above her tight butt. Tight round little butt divided by a visible line into two butterballs. How exactly do you get into pants like that? Well I just. He has never been particularly interested in the upper regions of girls. When she turns the corner of the building, he waits for a few moments before stepping into the unpleasant light.

MANNEQUIN MISCHIEF

The mannequin sees the man at the window, standing with his eyes closed. His lips and hands are pressed against the glass. She has seen this one before, looking up at her with his green, admiring eyes. Late at night the men sometimes gesture coarsely at her, try to attract her attention; once a man in a dark suit gravely bowed. It is all part of being a mannequin, a high instance of the art of appearance. The man at the window has always been respectful, an admirer, some sort of humble workman, perhaps. In the moonlight the mannequin feels her shoulders trembling. Her eyelids are moving, her fingers are quivering with life. She feels an inward streaming, and with a sense of fearful joy she turns her head slowly on her neck. At the window the man is opening his heavy-lidded eyes. The eyes, green as leaves under streetlamps, grow wider. The mouth begins to open. Now the man is moving backward, holding up both hands as if he is still pressing his palms against the glass. She feels the weight of her leg, turns her foot on her ankle. The man has struck his back against a telephone pole. The blow appears to startle him; his hands grope the air, then he is hurrying away, looking over his shoulder.

The mannequin, pleased by the sign of her power, begins walking up and down in the window space, stretching her long, slender legs, swinging her elegant arms. Now and then she stops to touch the cool glass, to feel a blue silk necktie or a folded shirt. When she turns she sees the moon-striped store behind her. In a moment she has stepped down from the window. She passes along an aisle lined with dresses and, holding out both arms, feels the dresses moving against her fingertips as the hangers jangle on the racks. The world is full of things to touch. She walks along a jewelry counter, running her fingers along the glass, moves among rich-smelling leather pocketbooks, silky rustling slips. On one counter a pair of moonlit legs, ending at the waist, stands in shimmering black pantyhose. On the counter across from it sits a faceless white head. The temptation is irresistible. The mannequin picks up the head, which is surprisingly light, crosses the aisle, and sets the head on the flat, slanted top of the legs. She stands back to admire her work. Slowly the head begins to slide, suddenly it falls, strikes the glass counter, drops to the floor, goes rolling bumpily away through stripes of moon and shadow. The mannequin is restless. There is nothing for her here. From a clattering rack she removes a lavender silk scarf and ties it around the calf of a solitary leg standing on a counter, bent at the knee. Impatiently she makes her way to the back of the store, where it is dark and windowless. Beside the shadowy shelves of boots and shoes she can make out a door. The door is heavy and opens with a sound of scraping metal. Cool night air moves against her face. Above the railroad embankment a black crisscross tower and moon-glittering black wires are sharp-etched against the blue-black sky.

WORDS HEARD
UNDER THE SPRUCES

"Look! Up there! There. See it?"
  "There?"
  "No, not there: there."
  "Oh, you mean…"
  "Yes! Yes! Isn't it…"
  "It's really very…"
  "Hello there, moon!"

LAURA IN THE THICKET

The moon has led Laura to a dense thicket in the rolling land between the back of the junior high school and the back of Denner's Body Shop. In the trees it's dark, with patches of moonlight. It reminds her of summer afternoons at Lake Quinnetuck, the sunspots on the pine needles, the smell of green. Laura feels soothed and excited in the trees, hidden and exposed. She feels the moon rippling all cobwebby across her arms and legs as she walks crackling through the dry needles. Her body feels feverish and cool. Moon, moon, do something. Save me. After a while she comes to a little clearing, a secret place: moon-blue sky above, moon-shade below, a patch of moonlight rippling along tree roots into deep shade.

In the small secret place, tree-walled, a little room among the trees, Laura steps into the patch of brightness and lifts her face to the moon. The moon is so bright she has to close her eyes. She stands with her face turned up, the way she's seen people in Indian summer, leaves yellowing on the trees, stand with their eyes closed and their bright faces turned to the sun. Her sun is the moon, feverish-cool. Ice-flames ride down her arms. She is a daughter of the moon. Touch me. Touch.

CHORUS OF NIGHT VOICES

Hail, goddess, night wanderer, sun-spurner. Hail, bright-sandaled one: watcher and dreamer, nighteye, downstreamer. You who soothe away day-sorrow, you friend of the outcast heart: touch, touch me now, burn me with brightness, pierce me with white arrows, till I am clean and clear as you, huntress and healer, all-revealer, comforter and destroyer.

HAVERSTRAW TAKES HIS LEAVE

Under the glare of the bare bulb over the door, Haverstraw hands Mrs. Kasco the wineglass.

"Coming in?" she asks, narrowing one eye against the smoke from the cigarette in her mouth. She removes the cigarette and lifts the back of a hand partway toward her mouth as she begins to yawn.

Haverstraw zips his windbreaker up to his throat, thrusts his hands in his pockets.

"It's getting on toward three," he says.

"Oh, three. I can manage."

"Well, I'm bad company now. I need to walk. Shake off this mood."

"You're all right?"

"I'll shake it off. You sleep now."

"Yes. Sleep. Listen. You hear them?"

"The grasshoppers?"

"Is that what they are?"

"Crickets, maybe. Cicadas. Who knows?"

"I've heard that sound my whole life. Even in Louisiana. Listen."

SONG OF THE FIELD INSECTS

By and by
Chk-a-chk mmmm
O by and by
Chk-a-chk mmmm

HOW TO LIVE

"The thing is," Haverstraw says, "you never see them. They're always there, but you never see them."

"I used to sit up late with my father on the big screened porch in back. Just the two of us, Daddy and me. He'd wear a suit and a white hat. Listen, he'd say. You hear that? That's the sound of the end of everything."

"Nice man."

"You remember that, he'd say. That will teach you how to live."

"And did it?"

"Hell no. But I always listen for it."

"I think they're crickets, probably. Some of them, anyway."

THE CRICKET
BLUEGRASS BAND

Live it up, live it up, live it up, live it up
Live it up, live it up, live it up, live it up

GOOD NIGHT

"Night now."

"Night."

Mrs. Kasco stands in the half-open doorway, holding her empty wineglass.

"You're all right?" she calls.

"I'm all right, all right. Right as rain. Right as night."

She raises her glass in salute.

"So: night."

"Night."

He raises an imaginary glass.

"To the night!"

"I'll drink to that."

She drinks.

"Night."

"Night."

LAURA INVISIBLE

Laura stands in the moonlight, eyes shut tight, feeling the whiteness burn into her. The moon sword is plunging deep, burning away her restlessness, cleansing her, killing her. She is drowsy and alert, fist-tense and half-swooning. She knows what she wants to do. Without opening her eyes, in the bright secret place, she takes off her denim jacket and lies down on her back. She slips her T-shirt over her head, tugs off her jeans—no underpants—and lies naked in moonlight. Free me, moon. Free me. The pine needles tickle her tense buttocks, her shoulders, the backs of her legs. The air is cool on her stomach. She wants to be consumed by moonlight. She thinks: this is insane, if anyone finds out. She thinks: I don't care I don't care I don't care. Then she lets go. Wrapped in light, invisible, she offers herself to the blazing moon.

DANNY IN THE BACK YARD

As he turns onto his street, Danny feels a weary restlessness. The street sign is missing from the top of the round metal pole. He lives on a no-name street in a nowhere town. The two-story frame houses sit looking at the steep thruway embankment like drugged-out ladies in an old-age home trying to remember what lies on the other side. He doesn't want to climb the stairs to his hot room, doesn't want to see the shirt on the back of the chair, the open window with its BB hole, the screen with a piece of Scotch tape over the rip. He knows the night view from his window too well: the solitary streetlight shining on nothing, the roof-high embankment with its dark trees, the trucks at the top rolling by, their headlights flickering through the spaces of the guard rail. No, better to walk around the front porch with the broken wicker loveseat, make your way along the rutted dirt driveway with its tufts of grass, and enter the back yard. Beside the porch steps lies the sloping cellar door, covered by a sheet of tin that glitters in the moonlight. A garbage can stands beside a hook hung with careless loops of hose. He's got to get the key back. From a pulley attached to a post of the small back porch, a clothesline stretches to a corner of the garage. Two white towels hang from the rope and cast black parallelograms on the grass. It embarrasses Danny to see underwear hanging on the line, his mother's slips and bras, his own white underpants. The kitchen window is dark, no one up at this late hour. Upstairs, in one of the windows of his parents' bedroom, a fan hums. His moon-shadow is sharp and clear along the grass. He can see dandelions in the moonlight, their jagged-toothed leaves, clumps of clover. Suddenly he lies down on his back in the grass, between the clothes-line and the towel-shadows. Big moon above, small town below. He's underneath the moon. Night pins him down. He'd like to wash away this whole evening, this whole life. He can hear the trucks rumbling on the thruway, the hum of the window fan, soft shrill of crickets, scrape of car tires on a road. The moon is looking down at him. A desire comes: to reach out and embrace the moon, to press it against his chest. O lady moon, up there in the sky. Wearily he closes his eyes.

DANNY'S SONG TO THE MOON

O lady moon, up there in the sky,
Won't you come down from your home so high?
Won't you come down?

If you come down before I die,
I'll give you rye whiskey and a slice of apple pie.

With a whang dang doodle dang dee.

VISITORS IN THE NIGHT

Past the shagbark hickory with the bird feeder shaped like a little house, past the wild cherry and the Japanese maple, along the fence with its three tall pussy willows and nine forsythias, down the row of zinnias at the edge of the vegetable garden, then along the latticework bottom of the back porch, past the garbage can, and up past the shagbark hickory with the bird feeder: so walks the woman who lives alone, on this summer night. She is wearing a pink summer bathrobe over her blue nightgown and she has placed a yellow zinnia in her hair. The grass is cool and soft on her bare feet, with hardness pushing up just underneath, but best of all are the round green hickory fruits that feel like little apples against her soles. In sunlight they look like tiny green pumpkins. The moonlight casts sharp shadows. She can see the long shadow of the bird feeder, like a witch's hat, the shadow-branches of the wild cherry, shadows of tomato sticks in the garden, her own long shadow rippling over grass. When she was a girl she had tea parties with her dolls under the summer moon, of course that was a long time ago. And suddenly she can't be sure. Would she have been allowed to do that? She remembers playing Statue, whirling round and round, falling in the green grass, one leg stuck up: don't move. She closes her eyes and begins to turn, holding out her arms, quickly she opens her eyes and looks around. It isn't at all the proper thing to do. What if someone's watching? And now she has spoiled it, it's time to go indoors: even a woman who lives alone must sleep, you know. She passes around the yard once more, climbs the steps of the back porch, enters through the kitchen door. There is bright moonlight in the kitchen. She passes into the darker living room and sees girls in the chairs. They have come to visit her, in the night. They are wearing black masks, they are rising like birds.

"Oh don't go," she cries, clasping her hands to her throat. "This is *such* a surprise. Won't you have some lemonade? Please. Please stay. This is such a nice surprise."

KISSES

He is kissing her hands, he is touching her face, the handsome one, the heartbreaker. In the blue summer night he burst through the hedge into her back yard. As he kisses her hands, as he touches her face, under the spruces—the smell of the spruces!—she remembers herself up in her room, behind the window, in some other life. He has broken the spell, released her into the night. He is kissing her hands, he is kissing her face. She can't see him now, he's all touch, the sly one, the heartstealer. Handsome is as handsome does. Who said that? Her mother said that. Oh what does it mean? Tell me what it means! He is kissing her mouth, slow nibbling kisses, kissable kisses. Nibble nibble little mouse. Who's that nibbling at my house? She is kissing his mouth, she is kissing his kisses. Kiss kiss. Oh yes. Yes yes. She is cracking apart. Flowers are bursting from her eyes. The night is making her insane. Why her? Why him? Steady, girl. Get a grip on yourself. She's seen it all a hundred times on TV, ho hum: good-looking guy, the fatal kiss, sorrow in suburbia. Her stupid hair! Touching her, kissing her. Who is he? Who? He is the night, he is what is. Bringer of night, spellbreaker, kissbringer, heartwringer. And she has the funny feeling that he's brought to her, right there in his pocket, all of the warm blue summer night: here, watch this: and with a toss of his hand, look!—the white moon, the blue sky, the rope swing, the smell of the spruces. He is kissing her mouth, she is falling into his mouth, she's feeling a little crazy, oh that's all right.

THE COMB

Behind the athletic field at the back of the junior high, the man with shiny black hair stands in the shadow of the bleachers. He is waiting for the girl in skintight jeans to emerge from the thicket. Thirteen minutes have passed and she is still in there. From his height at the back of the bleachers he commands a view of the moonwashed slope leading down to the trees and of the field stretching away beyond them to the back of Denner's Autobody. He has watched her walk into the trees and cannot understand what is delaying her. Is it possible that she? In there? Unzipping. Tugging. Crouching down: no one to see her. Dark. He steps out of blackness into brilliant moonlight and sees his shadow flung out in front of him like a spear. He hesitates and steps back. The light is not nice. From the pocket of his pants he takes out a silver comb and begins to comb his hair, following each stroke with a smoothing motion of his other hand.

COOP ALONG THE
RAILROAD TRACKS

Coop takes his own sweet time walking home along the alley between the storebacks and the railway embankment. He likes it back here, in no man's land, the stores in black shadow, embankment in bright moonlight. He's had six beers, maybe seven, eight at the most, nothing to write home about. Black iron gantries rise up over the tracks and look like black bridges against the sky. They're hung with power lines that glint in the moonlight. The streetlights back here are the old kind, the color of car headlights, not yet replaced by the new ones he's never liked, Kool-Aid orange. Fancy kind of name, chemical: boron, radon, tip of his tongue. In high school he used to walk the alley on hot summer nights, looking for girls, looking for trouble. Now he walks carefully, taking in the details. His vision of the mannequin moving in the window still shakes him and he wants to hold the world in place. Big metal garbage cans stand against the backs of the stores. Shadowy pipes and fat gas meters poke out of the walls near the ground. Now and then a space between stores opens up, giving a glimpse of lit-up store windows on the other side of Main Street. Barium-sulfur? On the bright side of the alley, staghorn sumac and tilted ailanthus trees grow among the stones on the embankment, up to the chainlink fence. Sodium-vapor: that's it. Coop passes the side of an iron gantry with a sign reading DANGER: LIVE WIRE. Beside the words is the drawing of a zigzag flash of lightning. Moonlight glitters on the brown glass insulators on the crossbars at the top. Trains in the night, the bright yellow windows, people going places, sharp-dressed women leaning back with half-closed eyes. Howl of the train whistle making your blood jump. Coop works in a body shop, hammering out dents and painting out rust. He does a little business on the side, restoring engines in the garage he shares with the noisy family living over him. The work tires him out; he wonders what else he might be doing. Summer after high school he drove a van for a moving company, nearly threw his back out. He needs a lucky break. There's a guy coming over tomorrow to pick up a Chevy that Coop hasn't even looked at yet. He needs his own business. He needs money in the bank. He's as fucking good as anybody else. He just needs a break. Just a little of the ready and in two three years he'll be living on Easy Street. Made in the shade. Way to go, Bill baby. William Cooper, 32 Easy Street, Dreamville, The Moon. Mr. William Cooper and Mrs. Isabel Amanda Cooper, formerly a mannequin, invite you to a dance party on Whitelawn Avenue, Moonhaven, Connecticut. Come as you aren't. Girls in white dresses dancing. In the fifth grade he had a pretty teacher called Miss Winterbottom and he spent the whole year thinking about her snowy white bottom. Coop looks up at the moon and it seems cold and far away. He stumbles and almost falls. He's breathing hard, his mind is turning. Eight beers was it, maybe nine. He remembers the old roller coaster, before it burned down. You could see it at night from the beach, hear the screams across the water. Girls in the cars, the first plunge, loving it. Carefully he crosses the alley and sits down against the back of a store between a garbage can and a gas meter. The crickets are going full tilt. He swears she moved in the window. On Main a car with the window down belts rock music into the night air and vanishes into some world of silence. Kids, summer, the smell of leather baseball gloves, the lazy good times: all gone. Gone the pretty girls in high school hallways, gone the quick smiles, the easy laughter. Summer nights sitting on the porch with Maureen O'Donnell, the creak of wicker, the clean smell of her skin. Only at night does it sometimes come back, the old feeling. Give me! Give! He'll check tomorrow, make sure she's there.

CHORUS OF NIGHT VOICES

Gone the pretty girls in high school hallways
Gone the white blouses, the laughter in back yards
Gone the night spins on the thruway in summer
Gone the old roller coaster, the prancing horses

PIERROT AND COLUMBINE

Released from the rigor of a single heartbroken attitude, Pierrot feels himself expanding into a multitude of melancholy poses, which will permit him to express the full poetry of his spurned and hopeless devotion. His Columbine, confined though she is to one unvarying expression of disdain, is so lovely that he wishes to fall continually at her feet in attitudes of adoration and ruin. But now, under the melting power of the moon, she has been set free to explore a rich repertoire of dismissive looks—the mocking, the bitter, the cruel, the reproachful, the laughing, the petulant, the defiant, the bored—accompanied by gestures eloquent with lofty indifference and delicate ennui. She is so beautiful in her refusals, so desirable in her moody fits and coy disdains, that Pierrot, even as he assumes a posture of despair, can long only to be provoked by her into yet more expressive revelations of humiliating and spirit-crushing desire; and as she sits crosslegged on the sill of the screened attic window, swinging one calf and gazing out with a bored demeanor at the nearly full moon, Pierrot catches her eye and in an instant, before she is able to glance wearily away, falls to his knees, holds out both arms, and bows his head gracefully in the attitude of one slain by love.

HAVERSTRAW IN MOONLIGHT

Haverstraw, unconsoled, takes the long way home. High under one arm he hugs a copy of *Jennie Gerhardt*, a book Mrs. Kasco has pressed on him, a book he isn't in the mood to read. Ever since he's known her she has lent him books, books that are supposed to increase his social consciousness. He squeezes the book against his side and walks on. He knows every road in this weary old dreary old town, knows the sites of Indian settlements, the seventeenth-century farms, the route the British took, shooting and burning, in 1779. He'd like to wipe it all out, start things over again, give the land back to the Indians. Or better yet, give it to him, to Haverstraw, King of the New World: trapper, hunter, fisher, farmer, sower of appleseed, stargazer, trailblazer, pathfinder, deerslayer, barefoot boy with cheek of tan, Huck Finn on the Housatonic, crackerbarrel philosopher, wily old coot in a coonskin cap, shrewd-eyed Yankee, inventor of the cotton gin, the printing press, the typewriter, founder of libraries, distributor of American jeans to the Indians, self-made tycoon in a thirty-room mansion, a hometown boy, worked his way up, one in a million, a lone ranger, a wayfaring stranger, a born loser, a man down on his luck. Haverstraw, sighing aloud, is startled by the sound. Soon he'll be muttering to himself, a spiteful old man without teeth. Chin-dribbler, slobberer. He is thirty-nine years old, a grown man living with his mother. He will never finish his book. Oh, a night of illuminations! Luminous moon, shine down on me! He is a failure. He ought to go out and get a job. You said it, buster. He repeats the litany of the jobs of his twenties: dishwasher at Sal's Home Cookin', short-order cook at Greasy Joe's, night clerk at the Cozy Moon Motel, bushtrimmer, leafraker, housepainter, waspkiller, driveway sealer, roof-gutter cleaner, private secretary to a retired professor writing a book on the teaching of mathematics in elementary school, delivery boy for a Chinese restaurant, attendant at a canoe-rental service at Lake Quinnetuck, actor (spook) for a Halloween hayride. Thirty-nine years old and nothing to show for it. Living off your mother, are you? Still stuck in the house he was born in. Oh, put a lid on it. Old, he's growing old. He can remember when mailboxes were olive green, stop signs yellow. Thirty-nine years old. He doesn't ask for much. A room, a pencil, a can of chicken soup. Ah, wilderness! A loaf of bread, a jug of wine, and forty thou. Grown-up men have money in the bank, mortgages, kids, wives, watchbands. What then am I? Haverstraw begins to enjoy it: I am a thirty-nine-year-old failure. I have based my life on a delusion. He is lost, lost—lost in the woods of himself—tangled up in his own undergrowth. No stars above: all dark. Grow up! Give it up! Haverstraw sighs again. Leave me be. He needs succor, heart shelter. Comfort me, night. Soothe me, old moon. The moon has betrayed him. Night has betrayed him. The night is nothing but a darker day. Haverstraw looks up, shakes his fist at the sky. He hates these streets, these smug houses. He decides to leave the beaten track, head home a wilder way. He can cut across the field in back of the junior high, pass through the trees, disappear for a while from the face of the earth.

CHORUS OF NIGHT VOICES

Hail, goddess, bright one, shining one: release him from confusion. Lighten his burden, banish his darkness: teach the sleeping heart to wake. Hail, goddess, night-enchantress: show the lost one the way.

THE CHILDREN
ENTER THE WOODS

Across moonlit back yards, under green badminton nets stretched between red-black metal poles, past sandboxes where yellow dump trucks cast long pointy shadows, under the spaces in white-flowering hedges, over lines of green-black hose attached to turned-off lawn sprinklers, around the corners of garages, past forgotten blue water pistols and jump ropes with red wooden handles, the children make their way toward the north part of town. There the streets become winding country lanes with a double yellow line down the center, bordered by short wooden posts with red reflectors. An occasional dead possum with a long pink tail lies at the side of the road. The music is louder now, more insistent. The children step over the thick twists of steel cable joining the brown posts and enter the woods. The ground crackles with pine cones and old leaves. Spots of moonlight lie on the tree branches and the forest floor. Sometimes the children stop, startled by a sound—a rabbit, maybe, or a raccoon—before continuing on their way. Can there be tigers in the woods? The music grows louder, clearer. Under the branches the children can feel the dark flute-notes streaming against them, caressing their skin.

DANNY AND THE GODDESS

On this clear summer night in southern Connecticut, the moon goddess sits on her throne. From her high seat she looks down on chimneys and rooftops, on the crossarms of telephone poles studded with glass insulators, on trucks rolling along the thruway. She looks down on gas tanks and water towers, on dark, small waves in Long Island Sound, on railroad tracks and white picket fences, on lifeguard chairs and sugar maples, on limestone quarries and pinewoods and the chutes of concrete plants, on high-voltage lines strung between steel pylons, on winding country lanes with a double yellow line down the center, on the individual winged fruits of a Norway maple on a quiet suburban street, on Danny lying asleep in his back yard between the clothesline and the garage. The lovely boy lies with his arms outspread and his face turned slightly to one side. The skin of his cheeks is smooth. Small blond hairs shimmer beneath his short dark sideburns and on the edges of his upper lip. Now the goddess mounts her silver chariot behind four milkwhite steeds, now she plunges through the night sky like a shooting star, her hair bright-streaming in the wind. Now the shining one swings down from her chariot and strides across the grass to where the lovely boy lies sleeping. Deep-smitten she looks at him, mortal and beautiful, young and dying. She sinks to her knees and caresses the fair face, peaceful in sleep. Never will she wake him, the sleep-enchanted: she will bind him in dream. Gently she undresses him, unclasps her mantle. Now she strokes the skin of the sleeping one, now she kisses his eyelids closed in dream, now she stiffens his love-lance with her hand. Now she rides him, the goddess astride him, takes him, the night-lovely one, even as he sleeps. Deep in his summer sleep, the earth-child lies dreaming. Bound in her spell, does he see the shining one who dropped through the night into his dream? Heart-stirred she rests, the goddess sharp-wounded. Then does she feel the melancholy of mortal love, for the children of earth are falling like mown grass even as they breathe. Earthbound she lingers there, the goddess love-burdened. Gently she clothes him, turns once to look at him, swiftly the bright-sandaled one mounts her chariot and rises into the night sky. In the grass of his back yard, on this clear summer night, Danny stirs in his sleep.

LIVING ROOM AND MOON

Through a pair of open curtains, moonlight enters the living room. The moonlight glistens on Laura's silver-speckled raspberry barrette lying on the mahogany piano bench, on the glass-covered black-and-white photograph, taken by her father, of a pile of lobster pots beside an overturned rowboat on the coast of Maine, on the blue porcelain statuette of a Chinaman standing on the coffee table, on a bronze key attached to a cowhide keycase resting on the arm of the reading chair beside the lamp table. Anyone sitting on the couch, head turned toward the screened window with the parted curtains, would see a basketball net over the garage door across the street, a roof with a black TV antenna against the dark blue sky, and a nearly full moon, white with blue shadows, divided into two uneven pieces by a single black antenna arm cutting across the bottom about a third of the way up.

UNDER THE SPRUCES

The famous moment has come, the young lovers naked under the spruces, moonlight, summer, and all that. He is amazed by his good luck, by her willingness, by the burst of serious feeling in himself, as if the dark blue summer night has entered him and is somehow working through him. As he moves slowly toward his ecstasy, approaching it but not quite there, not yet wanting to be there, he wonders suddenly, with surprise, what will break the heart more: the memory of the strangely grave lovemaking itself, on a summer night, under the spruces, or the memory of the way she swung out of shadow up into moonlight rippling across her legs and all at once let go: then she seemed to hang in the air, moon-glowing, mysterious, an emanation of the moon-dazzled summer night, before she moved downward, earthbound, heavy with love; the smell of the spruces; her head flung back; her hair; wild laughter under the moon.

DANCE OF THE DOLLS

In attics streaked by moonlight, the dolls begin to dance. Some dance with partners and some dance alone, at first slowly, then more rapidly, turning and turning, each in its fashion: the elephants dance an elephant dance, the tigers a tiger dance, the Raggedy Ann doll a floppy ragdoll dance, the one-eyed cuddly bear a cuddly bear dance, the porcelain-headed doll with blue glass eyes and black straw hat a stately minuet. A soldier in black busby and red jacket dances with Columbine, who flutters her eyelashes and looks away. Suddenly Pierrot springs from an old chair to the floor beside them. His loose white tunic with big white buttons and billowy sleeves flutters slowly to rest and hangs to his knees above his white pantaloons. His cheeks are flour-white, his eyes brilliant black. Drawing a toy dagger with a retractable blade, he plunges it into his heart. With both hands he seizes his chest, staggers a few steps, drops to one knee, gazes at Columbine, crumples to the floor. With a pert toss of her curls she dances off with the soldier, while Pierrot, lifting himself onto one elbow and resting one long hand languorously on a raised knee, gazes after her with bitter longing.

SONG OF THE ONE-EYED CUDDLY BEAR

I wuv woo. Does woo wuv me?

THE GARBAGE CAN

The mannequin in her peach-colored dress and dark green sunglasses walks along the railroad embankment on the moonlit side of the alley. She is exhilarated by her freedom, by the smell of the night, by the touch of the night air on her throat, and as she walks she swings her svelte arms, breathes deep through her narrow nostrils, and takes in, between the long and carefully curled lashes of her almond-shaped wide-spread eyes, every detail: the small flat stones on the slope of the embankment, the diamond-shaped spaces in the moon-glimmering fence, the black wires against the dark blue sky, a crushed blue-and-silver beer can gleaming among the stones. Once she stops to pick a dandelion on a tall stem. She carries it with her, twirling it in her slender fingers, inhaling its sharp, bracingly bitter fragrance. On the dark side of the alley, clusters of curving pipes stick out of the building near the ground. A shape is visible, and as she draws closer she sees it is a man. It is the man at the window, sitting against the wall beside a garbage can. His eyes are closed, but as she approaches they begin to open. He places one hand on top of the garbage can as if to push himself to his feet, while he continues to stare unmoving. The mannequin crosses the alley from moonlight to shade and stops in front of him. She looks down at the startled face looking up. Obeying a sudden impulse, she bends over and slips the stem of the dandelion into his coppery hair just above the ear. The man begins to struggle to his feet, pushing against the lid of the garbage can. His cheeks are streaked with tears. Standing at last with his back against the wall, he stares at her in confusion. She sees that he is shorter than she is. The dandelion hangs loosely from his hair. She reaches out a slender hand and touches his face.

She has never touched skin before, soft and silky over bone: her own hands and cheeks remain glass-hard. She takes his hand and they begin to walk slowly along the shadowy side of the alley. She can smell the leather of his jacket among the dark green scents of the embankment. When they step from shadow into moonlight she seems to feel, in her slender shoulders, the soft, silken weight of the moonlight sifting down.

DARK PARTY

Summer Storm, rising and clutching her pocket knife, sees that the lady is a little off. The signal to flee dies in her arm; she remains standing, wary, waiting.

"No lights," she commands.

"Of course not! On such a night! And look—the moon, in the window there. Oh how does it go? Why look, the moon ta tum ta tum...I can't remember..."

The girls are ready to get out of there, but they are also thirsty, and Summer Storm waits for the old bat to renew her offer. She seems to have forgotten all about them.

"You mentioned lemonade."

"Yes, I did, I certainly did. Don't you go away now. Lemonade for one two three four five yes. A very fine drink for a summer night."

From the kitchen they hear the sound of ice cubes dropping into glasses, liquid pouring, clinks of glass on glass.

She returns with a tray of glasses that she carries from girl to girl. She is smiling, this lady in the pink bathrobe with the crazy flower in her hair.

"Won't you sit down?" she says to Summer Storm, who shakes her head and remains standing as she takes a cool glass.

"And now I would like to say: welcome, young people. I was just taking a walk in the back and thinking how nice it would be, how very nice it would be. But you know, I'm a little out of practice, living out here and all, and if I've said or done anything wrong, please, I hope, I hope you will forgive me."

"Hey, it's all right," says Black Star.

"And now let me just put something on the Victrola."

In the dark she bends over a cabinet and removes a record.

Summer Storm wonders whether it's time to leave. The woman puts the record on the record player and stands motionless beside it as the tone-arm drops with a faint hiss. From where she stands, Summer Storm can see the record turning, the edge glittery black. The music takes her by surprise: it sounds like the kind of music you might hear on a merry-go-round, a sad and jaunty music, a wooden-horse tune shot through with the smell of cotton candy and the distant clatter of rides. In the moonlit dark living room she watches the loony lady begin to turn slowly, her arms outspread, her eyes half closed, her mouth smiling as she turns and turns on her bare feet on the dark rug with its pattern of peacocks.

PICTURES IN A GALLERY

As he enters the small woods behind the junior high, the man with shiny black hair is calm and excited. He is calm because he knows he will find her there, the young girl who should not be out alone so late at night, because didn't your mother ever tell you that it is not good no no to walk the streets at night in jeans so tight they are bound to attract the attention of strangers—the young girl destined to become part of his gallery. He is excited for three reasons: because he has already added two pictures today, because the third promises to be extremely stimulating, and because the hunt itself always has in it elements of excitement. Today in the library he felt certain that the blond-haired man in the tan trenchcoat lurking in the aisles was a detective trying to keep him from collecting exhibits, and even so he had collected two. In the oversized art books at the bottom of the Fine Arts section he kneeled down and saw, through the narrow, jagged space at the top of the books, a high school girl in black flats resting on her heels, facing him, looking for a book. She had thick yellow hair that came down over one shoulder of her white blouse and she wore a cream-colored skirt stretched tight across the tops of her big tan knees. One knee was slightly higher than the other. As she moved a little in search of a book, reaching, throwing her hair back with one hand, the two knees would come apart and suddenly press together, now you see it now you don't, open and shut case, little yellow hairs on her legs, what did she think she, teasing him, taunting him, the little slut. Later, kneeling at the bottom shelf in Biography, he saw a heavy-set sickly-pale girl with black down on her cheeks sitting on the floor of the aisle opposite, facing him with her back against the shelves. Studious type: absorbed in a book. She sat with raised knees pressed together—so demure!—ankles apart, black skirt pulled tightly over pale knees, revealing a vista of fish-white underthighs and a pink bulge of underpants while she twirled a hank of black hair round and round a plump finger. These were fine exhibits, but the blond-haired man in the tan trenchcoat was making him nervous and he left the library shortly after. Now, as he enters the woods, he is certain that the girl in skintight jeans, who should not be walking alone in deserted places, even on a fine summer night, will provide him with more leisurely, more irresistible pleasures.

COOP AND HIS LADY

It's all the same to Coop whether he's hallucinating or not: his lady has come down to him, and they're walking hand in hand along the railroad embankment, on this summer night. There's nothing at all except the now of this night. Come morning he'll chalk it up to drink and dream, but now it's all as real as the tilt of her hat and the scratch of gravel under his heels. She's alive but not flesh-alive, not skin-and-bone alive, and he likes her that way: she's perfect in her mannequin beauty, flawless, lofty-cool. He loves her but doesn't desire her, or rather he desires her but doesn't need to fulfill his desire—he desires only to continue desiring her, this night-lady with her glass-smooth arms and the glint of moonlight on her neck. Her dress, which looks soft as tissue paper, shakes over her long legs as she walks. Her small and perfect breasts look firm as polished stones. He wonders whether the breasts of mannequins have nipples, he once read something somewhere, and as he tries to imagine the smooth, cool, unnippled breasts of his lady, he no longer knows whether he's attracted by the little-girl innocence of her ice-smooth body or by its exotic, corrupt seductiveness. He wonders what she's wearing under there, maybe bra and panties so silky-delicate that the mere act of looking at them would tear them. He's having strange thoughts, old Coop is. He feels way up there, lifted out of himself, crazed. He sees that what really moves him about his lady isn't her sudden touchable nearness but her untouchable, out-of-this-world thereness, her unshakable unreality. It strikes him that his fleshiness is probably interesting to her, as it might not be if she were entirely human. This thought, which might have disturbed him on some other night, deeply pleases him on this night that's like no other; and with a burst of pleasure he pulls her closer, inhaling her subtle perfume that reminds him somehow of summer snow.

AN ENCOUNTER

Haverstraw, stepping out of moonlight into the shelter of the trees, has the sense that he is eluding pursuit. He isn't soothed, precisely, but for a moment he feels safe from the mockery of the moon. Creep out of sight: never come out. He has to make his way carefully here, else he'll trip over a root, hit his head on a branch for sure. Conk his coconut. Bonk his bean. He makes his way cunningly, Chingachgook, through darkness broken by bits of moonlight. This is the forest primeval. The murmuring pines and the—. He hears something up ahead like a crackle of footsteps and sees a figure moving through the trees. He thinks of calling out, but holds back: it's around three in the morning and there's something about the shadowy form he doesn't like. The other isn't really walking through the moon-spotted dark, but seems to be creeping slowly forward. Haverstraw thinks of the cat he saw earlier in the summer, creeping up on a grackle. It occurs to him that he might end up with a knife in his gut. Is that what he's been looking for? Disaster, death, the end of desk-sorrow. Smash it up, bash it up. Even so he moves cautiously. The figure is a man, angular, smallish. Haverstraw, no fighter, is big-shouldered, soft, and tall. He creeps after the creeper: hunters in a wood. The creeper crouches down suddenly, parts a branch. At that moment Haverstraw sees a clearing, moonlight, something lying there: a girl, asleep or dead.

"Hey!" calls Haverstraw, stepping forward. He raises *Jennie Gerhardt* over his head, ready to hurl it like a rock.

The man jerks his head over his shoulder, leaps up, half falls, runs stumbling through the trees.

The naked girl is screaming, trying to cover herself with her hands.

"He's gone," Haverstraw says, violently averting his face, stepping into the moonlight.

He turns his back, puts down the book, tears off his windbreaker. He holds out the jacket stiffly behind him, tosses it in her direction.

"I'll stand guard. It's all right. Calm down. That creep didn't see you. Easy. Shhh. He's gone. It's all right now. Really."

Behind him he hears a crazed scrambling. He wants to comfort her, but how? Don't look. He hopes the small man comes back, he'd like to smash his head into a tree. Somehow the man had known she was here. A young girl, taking off her clothes. Crazy stuff. He himself saw her for a second, thin and white, little breasts. Ah, her shame!

"I don't think he's coming back," Haverstraw says. "You all right?"

When he turns around he sees that she's gone. Of course! A vision in the night. He feels a sharp burst of disappointment. In the grassy clearing, bright in the moonlight, his dark blue windbreaker lies with one arm straight out, like a policeman in an old movie. Something small is resting on the jacket.

He steps over and picks up a half roll of Life Savers. The open end is crumpled, the silver paper torn; the striped paper covering the rest of the roll is smooth and glossy. He can imagine a number of explanations—it might have fallen out of her pocket, for example—but he prefers to think of it as her gift to him. He continues to study it in the light of the moon, then puts it in his shirt pocket and gives it a pat.

For thirty minutes by his strapless watch, which he holds in one hand, Haverstraw stands guard in the clearing, pacing in the moonlight, looking in all directions, listening. Then he picks up his windbreaker and Mrs. K's book and heads for home.

THE PIPER IN THE WOODS

Dark and sweet, dark and sweet, the night-notes draw the children deeper into the woods, past tree trunks fat as elephant legs, under branches that run like ink against the blue night sky: runny ink branches and elephant trees, and the scrapy roots and the scritch-scratch leaves. The moon is cut by little black twigs. The moon's a cracked dinner plate. Whisperers move behind every tree. That tree's a skeleton: it'll hug you to death. Look! A witch tree. Dead man's tree. What's that? Shhh. Who's there? Sharp and deep, sharp and deep, the night music calls. Through the moony woods move the mum children, dark children rippling with spots of moon. Louder, clearer: the rising and falling sharp-sweet music brushes against the skin of their cheeks, touches their hands and faces, passes through them and comes out the other side. An opening in the trees, and there in the clearing, on a small rise, standing in the ankle-deep grass, turning, bending his body, playing a dark flute, a strange man with naked chest and sharp ears, hairy flanks and prancing goat-legs. He turns and turns, bending almost to the grass, rising high, a moon-dancer, a flute-dreamer, as the children gather in the clearing to listen to the dark, sweet music of the piper in the woods. They must have this music. It's the sound of elves under the earth, of cities at the bottom of the sea. In the clearing the children listen, their lips slightly parted, their eyes veiled and heavy-lidded.

DANNY WAKING

Danny, waking, looks for the chair with the shirt over the back and the window with the BB hole. He can't understand the towels hanging down, the dark blue air, the hardness under him. It all comes clear. He sits up, rubs his neck. He remembers lying down in the yard, the shadows of the two towels. The shadows have moved, they're almost up to the side of the garage. Time to go in and sleep. His neck hurts, his back is stiff, but he feels better—his little moon-nap has done him good. Dim memory of a white dream, fading, ungraspable: vanished. He'd better get up to his room, crawl into bed before his parents catch him out here, another crazy teenager, lock him up. Father, I cannot tell a lie. I chopped off his head with my own ax. He can hear the trucks on the thruway and the hum of insects and somewhere another sound, a faint electrical crackle, tsst tsst, probably from the streetlight below his front window. Danny recalls the library break-in, the words with Blake—it all seems long ago. He's feeling really pretty good. Things will work out. He loves the summer, warm nights stretching on forever, long walks alone, the yellow windows, girl-thoughts, streetlights shining through leaves. Patience. His time will come. He stands up, takes a deep breath, looks up at the moon. As if someone is watching him, he places a hand on his stomach and grandly bows. Lady moon, we thank you. Keep up the good work. Danny turns and heads for the front porch.

A LITTLE CHANGE

Hand in hand she walks with him along the railroad embankment, past telephone poles with aluminum numerals screwed into the wood, past milkweed pods, past storebacks and garbage cans. When they pass under streetlights their shadows stretch out longer and longer in the pools of yellowish light but never disappear entirely: another shadow, a moon-shadow, creeps out from the first, at another angle. She feels the change at first in her arms, not as a stiffness or coldness, but as a slight loss of ease, a motion in the direction of her mannequin nature. So it has come. She looks up over the store roofs and sees a faint streak of gray in the sky. On the embankment side, the sky over the chainlink fence remains radiant deep dark blue. Secretly she has known it must come. She must return to her window, she must again assume her pose, the pose she can already feel within her, working its way outward toward fulfillment: one arm slightly raised, the fingers gracefully extended, the eyes half closed behind her fashionable sunglasses. But now, as she walks between two worlds, on this summer night when the moon has released her, she is shaken with gratitude.

YOUNG

He has covered her with his shirt, he is kissing her hands, the lovely one, the heartbreaker, and still the night goes on, the impossible summer night that can never end, for this is the way it has always been, here in the secret place, under the spruces. For the night that is once is the night that is always, and now is the only eternity that will ever be. Oh god, she's having wild thoughts, dream thoughts under the summer moon. She can feel the night working through her, she is a daughter of the night and the moon and her hair is streaming in the branches of the trees and her breath is the night sky. She is happy, happy, she wants to cry out with happiness. But already in the center of her happiness Janet feels a faint distraction, a tug of day-thoughts: must be going in before too long, hair appointment at eleven, beach at two. She thrusts the pesky voice away and breathes deep, as if she is trying to breathe in all of the summer night with its smell of spruce needles and the cry of the crickets and the soft sound like a rustle that is the sound of the trucks on the far thruway. Like a prince he came to her, asleep in her tower. Well not asleep exactly, but anyway. He is kissing her hands, even now. Gravely she thinks: this is what I will remember. Through the spruce branches she can see a glowing piece of moon. She has the odd sense that she's up there, looking down, remembering. She is remembering that summer night long ago when he kissed her hands under the spruces, back in the days when she was young, when she was wild, when anything was possible in the night never ending.

CHORUS OF NIGHT VOICES

This is the night of the smell of spruces. This is the night of the handsome one bursting through the high hedge. This is the night of the princess waking in the thornwood. O you who wait: this is the night of the opening of the heart.

COOP ALONE

Coop, weary, walks home alone along the railroad tracks. His head is clear now, pretty clear, not too clear but a little clearer. He remembers the change in her, the tilt of her head different, as if she were listening to something far away. Hurried leavetaking. Did she touch his face, under the streetlight? He wishes he'd gone after her, instead of standing there like a lunkhead watching her walk away, a bright lady fading into shadow on the dark side of the alley. It's all fading into shadow now. He's no longer sure whether he kissed her under the streetlight, though he remembers the sharp reflection of the light in each lens of her sunglasses and the shimmer of yellow light on her throat. In the morning it will be something else, Coop's dream of a summer night. But now as he heads for home along the tracks he believes in this clear summer night, when the lady of his desire came down to him from her high window, and took his hand and walked with him along the railway embankment, like a visitor from some unknown place— deeper than dream, more dangerous than desire—sent to soothe him on his way.

THE WOMAN WHO LIVES ALONE
SHOWS A TOUCH OF CUNNING

The girls have melted into the night, and the woman who lives alone is standing at the sink in her moonlit kitchen, washing the lemonade glasses. When she leans forward against the sink, she can see a piece of moon through the upper left pane of the dark window. She is remembering their names: Summer Storm, Black Star, Night Rider, Paper Doll, Fast Lane. The names thrill her, like secrets whispered in her ear. She has the sense, when she recites the names, that she is tearing off the black masks. Out of the night they came to her, the five dearies. Ah, but she was cunning: she pretended not to know who they were. And yet she has read about them in the paper, the girls who roam through the night, breaking into houses. She has thought about them. She has imagined them. No one has ever seen them before. But now she has seen them, in their black masks, the dear ones, the daughters. She has learned their names: Summer Storm, Black Star, Night Rider, Paper Doll, Fast Lane. She will never reveal their secret. She feels they feel she understands them, and she does: they cannot stay in their rooms alone, they cannot, cannot, they must go out into the night and never be known. Because when you are known, then you lose yourself, but when you are hidden, then you are free. Summer Storm, Black Star, Night Rider, Paper Doll, Fast Lane. As the woman who lives alone dries a glass, dark-shining in the light of the night sky, she has an inspiration: she will take a name for herself. And the name comes, as if it has always been waiting to be summoned: she will call herself SISTER OF THE SUMMER MOON. For the moon has been good to her, the moon has brought her visitors, on this lovely summer night. She begins to hum to herself, as she dries a glass in the dark kitchen glimmering with moonlight.

HAVERSTRAW WALKING HOME

Haverstraw, walking home, feels refreshed after his little adventure. He worries about the girl, he'd have liked to soothe her, calm her down, but her gift reassures him: she understands that the night has rewarded her with rescue, not harm. She had taken off her clothes and fallen asleep in the clearing, in the light of the moon. Diana the huntress: chaste and fair. Protectress: guardian of virgins. He then was the emissary of the moon. Haverstraw, punisher of spies. He casts a sidelong glance at the moon, surprised to find her lower in the sky. Moonrise and moonset, east to west. It never feels that way: she seems to sit there, never moving. He winces, remembering how he irritated Mrs. Kasco. Ad for eternity. Wise guy. Well, he takes it back. Goddess, forgive me. Mercy on us poor clowns. Under this shiteating greasepaint grin is a mouth of sorrow. Haverstraw thinks of the girl's moonlit white body and quickly averts his inward gaze. He reaches up to his shirt pocket, pats the Life Savers to make sure they're still there. The man probably wouldn't have done anything, his pleasures were more private than that, but you never could tell. *Jennie Gerhardt* would have laid him out cold. Good heft, hard binding: a brick of a book. Jennie to the rescue. Social value of art. Mrs. K will enjoy the story. He's glad the goddess chose him to play his part, on this adventurous night. Now he wants to get to bed. There's work to be done tomorrow. He's a thirty-nine-year-old failure with a skewed life, a clown and a wise guy and a born loser, a flab-bellied bachelor with no prospects, but if he can just get to his desk then somehow it will be all right, he asks no more. Oh, he asks more, much more, but on this night, night of the almost full moon, night of Diana the huntress, he asks only for a little light along the way. The night sky clear, a touch of gray in the east.

COLUMBINE

Fresh from her flirtation with the soldier, who already bores her to
death, Columbine walks with a swish of skirts and a flutter of her
fan past old trunks, a tripod without a camera, a dusty baseball
glove holding a grass-stained baseball, into an unknown part of the
attic. Here great barrels loom. She does not know what she is looking for. She wishes to be alone, everything bores her to distraction,
but at the same time she wishes to be pursued, if only for the
pleasure of scorning the pursuer. As she rounds a barrel she sees
something on the floor: it is a figure sprawled on the ground, dis-
gustingly drunk no doubt. But at once she recognizes the loose
blouse and the balloon sleeves. He is lying on his back, his head
turned to one side, one arm outstretched and the other crossed
over his chest. A line of moonlight lies across his throat like a bright
scar. Beside the fingers of the outstretched hand lies a gun.
Columbine hesitates. She does not like difficulties. Can the imbe-
cile finally have done what he has always threatened to do? Irrita-
bly she prods the figure with her foot. It is like pushing against a
sack of flour. Pierrot's attentions irk her, his very existence puts her
nerves on edge, but she is used to him and does not relish the
absence of opportunities for disdain. She bends over, shakes his
shoulder harshly, lifts and lowers the limp hand on his chest. She
kneels beside him, touches his cheek. Limp, dead: in death he is
almost beautiful. Something stirs in her, deep down. "Please," she
whispers, stroking his face. Pierrot's eyes spring open, he stares at
her mournfully. "Idiot!" she cries. She leaps to her feet, looks furi-
ously down at him, and strides off into the dark, though not before
glancing at him over her shoulder. Pierrot, his cheek warm from her
touch, watches her swish around a corner, then rises nimbly to his
feet and sets off in doleful pursuit.

DAWN

Now the dawn goddess in the palace of the East rises wearily from her couch, rubs her eyes, and puts on her saffron robe. She hurries to the courtyard, where she mounts her silver-wheeled chariot. Swiftly the two horses rise into the air, scattering darkness. At the first glimmer of gray in the sky, the piper in the woods looks up, bends and spins once more, and breaks off abruptly. In the shocking silence he beckons toward the sky, then turns and vanishes into the woods. The children, waking from their long dream, look around tiredly and head for home. The outlaws in their black masks have already slipped back into their own houses, hidden their masks in closets or bureau drawers, and pulled the covers over their shoulders. Janet looks down once more into the yard where her lover waves one more time before disappearing through the hedge. Now the dolls are growing sluggish, their limbs are stiffening. Pierrot cannot lower the white arm that reaches toward Columbine, whose lovely body, straining away from him, can no longer flee. The one-eyed cuddly bear sits motionless against a nearby trunk. Haverstraw's mother wakes for a moment as the front door clicks shut, then falls deeply asleep as she hears his footsteps climbing the stairs. Laura, closing the door to her room, hopes the man understood that she has thanked him. On a moonlit rug with a pattern of peacocks lies a yellow zinnia. Danny is fast asleep despite the noise of trucks coming through the screen of the open window. The guys in the library have left long ago. Coop lies dreaming and waking, tossing in his sheets, while in the window of the department store the mannequin stands stiffly in her straw hat and sandals, gazing out at the stoplight changing from red to green. In her bedroom on the second floor, Mrs. Kasco lies fast asleep, though the insects are loud through her open window. The lovers and loners have left the beach, over the dark water a thin band of sky has grown pale, gulls walk in the seaweed and straw of the tide-line, the moon, nearly full, shines in the part of the sky where it is still a summer night.

About the Author

Steven Millhauser is the winner of the Pulitzer Prize for *Martin Dressler*. He is the author of eight previous books, including *Edwin Mullhouse*, *Little Kingdoms*, and *The Knife Thrower*, among other books.